MAN OF STEEL™

THE EARLY YEARS
JUNIOR NOVEL

HarperFestival is an imprint of HarperCollins Publishers.

Man of Steel: The Early Years
Copyright © 2013 DC Comics.
SUPERMAN and all related characters and elements are trademarks of and © DC Comics.
WB SHIELD: TM & © Warner Bros. Entertainment Inc.
(s13)

HARP29865
Printed in the United States of America. No part of this book may be used or reproduced in any
manner whatsoever without written permission except in the case of brief quotations embodied
in critical articles and reviews. For information address HarperCollins Children's Books,
a division of HarperCollins Publishers, 10 East 53rd Street, New York, NY 10022.
www.harpercollinschildrens.com
Library of Congress catalog card number: 2013932627
ISBN 978-0-06-223604-3
Typography by John Sazaklis
13 14 15 16 17 LP/BR 10 9 8 7 6 5 4 3 2 1
❖
First Edition

MAN OF STEEL™
THE EARLY YEARS
JUNIOR NOVEL

Adapted by Frank Whitman

Inspired by the film MAN OF STEEL
Screenplay by DAVID S. GOYER
Story by DAVID S. GOYER and CHRISTOPHER NOLAN

SUPERMAN created by JERRY SIEGEL and JOE SHUSTER

HARPER FESTIVAL
An Imprint of HarperCollinsPublishers

™

PROLOGUE

The earthquake struck without warning.

One minute it was a sunny spring day in downtown Metropolis. Throngs of people crowded the busy sidewalks and outdoor cafes. Honking trucks and taxis fought the lunch-hour traffic. People talked on cell phones as they waited at crosswalks or walked their dogs. A monorail zipped by on an elevated track. A sidewalk vendor hawked hot dogs and cold sodas from his cart. An open beach umbrella protected him from the bright sunlight.

"Hot dogs!" he called out to passing pedestrians. "Two for the price of one!"

A minute later, a powerful tremor shook the city. A low rumble rose up from deep within the earth, quickly drowning out the everyday clamor of the street. Towering skyscrapers swayed back and forth like trees in the wind. Startled pedestrians stumbled atop the quaking pavement, losing their balance. They grabbed street lamps and newspaper kiosks to keep from falling. Frantic dogs yapped and tugged at their leashes. Dust and soot fell from the ledges of quivering buildings. A dislodged air conditioner crashed to the sidewalk, narrowly missing a woman pushing a cart full of flowers.

"Whoa!" the hot dog vendor exclaimed. His name was Tony, and he had been selling hot dogs on this corner since he was old enough to work. He had never felt anything like this before. "What on earth—?"

He held on tightly to his cart, which was shaking like a washing machine on its spin cycle. A tray of boiled frankfurters slid off the top of the cart onto the sidewalk. Mustard and ketchup bottles crashed to the pavement, which rattled beneath Tony's feet. At first he had thought that maybe it was just a subway train passing below him, but the unnerving vibration grew in intensity, until he realized what was happening.

It was an earthquake!

Scared people ran for cover all around him, seeking shelter in doorways and subway entrances. Cars and trucks slammed on their brakes, rear-ending each other. The crash of colliding metal added to the chaos. Shouts and screams erupted from the panicked people fleeing the streets. Tony wanted to join them, but was afraid to leave his cart unattended.

He waited a minute too long.

A truck driver lost control of his vehicle. The large delivery truck swerved toward the sidewalk, jumping the curb. The driver honked his horn urgently as the truck barreled toward Tony and his cart. Brakes squealed, but couldn't stop the truck in time. Tony froze in terror as he saw the ten-thousand-pound truck bearing down on him.

"Help," he whispered. "Help me, please!"

Suddenly a caped figure dropped from the clear blue sky and landed on the pavement right in front of the oncoming vehicle. A bright red "S" was displayed proudly on the man's broad chest. His skintight blue uniform and long red cape were world famous. The cape fluttered in the breeze as he stood confidently between Tony and the truck, unafraid of the runaway vehicle speeding toward him.

Tony's eyes widened in recognition. His jaw dropped.

"Superman!" he blurted.

Everyone in Metropolis knew about the Man of Steel, but Tony had never seen Superman up close before. Once or twice, he had spied a blue-and-red blur streaking through the sky above the city, but that was as close as he had ever come to actually laying eyes on the world's greatest super hero. Hope flared in the young man's chest.

"It's okay," Superman said. "You're safe."

The truck headed straight for Superman, who didn't look at all worried by the rushing vehicle. He threw out his arms and stopped the truck with his bare hands. Metal crumpled loudly as the truck slammed to a halt, as though it had smashed into a brick wall. An airbag exploded in the cab, protecting the driver from the impact. Steam escaped the mangled hood of the truck.

Superman was unhurt by the collision, which hadn't even budged him. He scanned the driver with his X-ray vision to make sure he hadn't been seriously injured, and didn't see any broken bones beneath the man's skin. Superman stepped back from the demolished truck and checked on Tony as well.

"Are you okay?" Superman asked.

"I think so, yes," the amazed vendor said. "Thanks to you, Superman!"

Superman nodded. Confident that both the driver and the vendor were safe for now, he launched himself into the sky like a rocket. The earthquake was still going on, and he was needed elsewhere. The trick was going to be figuring out where he could do the most good while the whole city was shaking.

Defying gravity, he flew over Metropolis, soaring higher than the city's many tall skyscrapers. He had been on a routine patrol of the city when the earthquake had hit, endangering persons and property for miles around. He had already rescued several people, including a couple of falling window washers, but he knew that was just the beginning. He could still hear a rumbling deep within the earth's crust, as well as people crying out in fear and distress all over Metropolis.

This was definitely a job for Superman.

His super-hearing alerted him to a sudden loud crack. Glancing down, he saw a carved stone gargoyle break off from the top of a four-story brick apartment building. The grotesque ornament plummeted toward the sidewalk below, where a petrified jogger was clinging to a lamp pole for dear life. She had no idea that she was about to be crushed by a falling gargoyle.

But Superman saw her danger—and knew what to do.

His eyes glowed red, like burning coals, and a pair of crimson beams shot from his eyes. The beams converged on the gargoyle, detonating the solid stone with a single blast, so that only ashes rained down on the jogger, who looked up in surprise to see a caped figure streaking away at super-speed.

That was close, Superman thought. *Too close.*

Scanning the shaking city from above, Superman spotted an even bigger potential tragedy. A stretch of elevated track, running two stories above the streets below, had collapsed several blocks away. A speeding monorail, carrying dozens of commuters and tourists, was heading straight for the open gap in the track. Sparks flared as the train's operator leaned on the brake, but the monorail had too much momentum. It was only seconds away from going over the edge—and crashing nose-first into the street.

Unless Superman got there in time.

Pouring on the speed, he dived down from the sky

and flew beneath the train, catching it just as it sped off the tracks into the empty air. Screams of terror turned into cheers and applause inside the train as Superman lifted it above his head and kept it from crashing.

"Got you," he said.

He looked around for someplace to put the train down safely. Because he didn't trust the crumbling tracks, he carried the train thirty blocks north to Centennial Park, where he gently deposited it in the middle of a large, grassy field. Startled bystanders gaped in amazement, despite the ground trembling beneath their feet. Superman hurried around to the side of the train and tore open an emergency exit with his bare hands. The people inside the cars looked dazed, but intact.

"End of the line," Superman said. "Everybody out."

By now, the earthquake was beginning to subside, but Superman knew his work wasn't done yet. Leaving the grateful riders behind, he shot up into the air and once again inspected Metropolis from above.

Heaps of rubble littered the streets and sidewalks. Smoke and flames rose from gaping cracks in the pavement, some of which were big enough to swallow entire cars and buses. Shaken people were nervously emerging from shelter, gazing around in confusion and dismay. Police cars, fire trucks, and ambulances raced to deal with the aftermath of the quake. Spinning red lights flashed on top of the emergency vehicles, while sirens blared across the city.

Metropolis looked like a disaster area. Superman knew the devastation could have been much worse, but it was still a troubling sight. The widespread devastation reminded him of an even greater cataclysm, many years ago, and the long, winding journey that had led to him becoming Superman.

A journey that had begun on an alien planet many light-years from Earth. . . .

CHAPTER ONE

"I can't! I can't go through with it!"

Lara Lor-Van cradled her newborn baby in her
arms. She was a beautiful, dark-haired woman wearing
an elegant gown of genetically engineered silk. She
held on tightly to the baby boy while pacing inside an
observatory on the planet Krypton. The observatory was
located within a domed citadel atop a steep black cliff
that overlooked an alien wilderness filled with strange,
exotic beasts. An aging red sun was setting outside

as she pleaded with her husband, Jor-El, their world's greatest scientist. The family crest of the House of El was printed on the chest of his dark blue skinsuit. It looked like the letter "S."

"We have no choice, Lara," he said gently. "Krypton is doomed."

Their planet was home to an advanced scientific civilization. The people of Krypton had thrived for hundreds of thousands of years, but when their society began to run out of energy, they had foolishly tapped into the core of their own planet, triggering a dangerous chain reaction. Jor-El had tried to warn his fellow Kryptonians of the danger, but they'd refused to listen to him. Nobody wanted to believe that the entire planet was going to explode soon.

"This starcraft is Kal-El's only chance," Jor-El reminded Lara. "I've found a new world for him, where the people look very much like we do. But that planet's yellow sun will fill his cells with energy. He'll be stronger and faster and more indestructible than anyone else on the planet." He reached for the baby. "He'll be *safe*, Lara."

"Wait!" she protested. "Not yet! Just a while longer."

"There's no time, Lara. We have to say good-bye."

He took the baby from his wife and placed Kal-El inside a space capsule of his own design. The experimental starcraft was the size and shape of a large boulder, with rounded edges like the shell of some gigantic marine animal. He and Lara had raced against time to construct the craft, which was just big enough to carry Kal-El into space. There was no room for Jor-El or Lara. They would have to stay behind to perish with their world.

But their son would survive.

Jor-El's heart was breaking, too. He didn't want to say good-bye to their child any more than Lara did, but there was nothing else they could do. Krypton's time was running out. Violent tremors and volcanic eruptions were tearing the planet apart, even as the High Council continued to deny the truth.

"Sleep, my son," he said. "Our hopes and dreams go with you."

He placed a small black object into the cradle with the baby. The object resembled a polished black spike or nail, with their family crest inscribed on its head. In theory, this command key would someday help Kal-El discover his Kryptonian heritage.

Jor-El wished he could see the man Kal-El would grow up to be.

An earthquake shook the citadel. Dust and debris rained down from the domed ceiling. Jor-El stumbled and almost lost his balance. He grabbed hold of a console to steady himself. Lara gasped.

"It's happening," she said, "just as you predicted."

He nodded grimly. "The tremors are increasing in intensity. The chain reaction is building. Soon the entire planet will blow apart." He double-checked to make sure the starcraft's propulsion and life-support systems were online and functioning properly. Helper robots prepared the craft for launch. "There is no time to lose," Jor-El said.

A hatch closed automatically, sealing the baby

inside the protective capsule, which filled with a clear organic gel that would insulate the baby from the dangers of space. Lara joined Jor-El, and they hugged each other as the starcraft pivoted into position. Its nose tilted upward toward an open gap in the ceiling, which revealed Krypton's fading red twilight. They reached together for a control panel and triggered the final launch sequence.

"Good-bye, Kal-El," his mother said. "Be safe."

Thrusters along the bottom of the starcraft lit up, glowing more brightly than the sun. The craft rocketed into the sky, heading for the stars. Jor-El and Lara watched it climb toward space until it was only a tiny glowing speck in the sky. Within moments, the speck disappeared in the distance.

Another earthquake, even stronger than before, rattled the observatory. Jor-El knew that the final disaster was beginning. Enormous volcanoes were erupting all over the planet, spewing bright green lava. Entire cities would be engulfed in a burning sea. Soon the whole globe would explode into pieces. All that would be left of Krypton would be chunks of radioactive rubble drifting in space. Jor-El and Lara had launched the starcraft just in time.

Krypton was dying, but their son would live— somewhere on a distant world.

TM

CHAPTER TWO

The starcraft hurtled through space. It sped across the universe through the endless, empty darkness between the stars. Its hard outer shell protected the craft from the hazards of deep space: asteroids, comets, solar flares, and cosmic radiation. Special engines, devised by Jor-El, let it cross vast distances many times faster than the speed of light, while little Kal-El slept peacefully inside his protective capsule. The blast that had destroyed Krypton had briefly shaken the capsule, but Kal-El had not been harmed.

The baby had no idea of the amazing life in store for him.

In time, the starcraft approached its destination: a distant solar system many light-years away from the shattered remains of Krypton. Several planets orbited a bright yellow star that was less than five billion years old. The craft passed the system's outer planets, including a large ringed giant, and made it safely through a crowded asteroid belt before closing in on the third planet from the sun. The blue-green world was largely covered in water, but boasted several large continents and a pair of white polar ice caps. Its cloudy, oxygen-rich atmosphere, although different from Krypton's, was capable of supporting life. Its brilliant yellow sun was younger and hotter than the aging red star that had witnessed Krypton's destruction. The yellow sun bathed the planet with light and warmth. Plant and animal life was abundant on this strange new world, whose inhabitants called it . . . Earth.

The starcraft slowed, dropping out of light speed, as it neared the planet. Still traveling at thousands of miles an hour, it zipped past the planet's solitary moon and entered Earth's atmosphere. The heat of friction caused the space capsule to glow red-hot, but its fireproof shell protected the baby inside. Plunging through the clouds, the computerized vessel came in for a landing over the middle of a large continent in the northern hemisphere of the planet. Wide-open plains offered an ideal landing site.

Kal-El's long journey was almost over—and his new life was about to begin.

"Look at that, Jonathan."

Jonathan Kent looked to see what his wife, Martha, was pointing at. They were driving home to their farm in Kansas, after picking up groceries and supplies in the nearby town of Smallville. It was a clear autumn night, and the sky was full of stars, but he quickly spotted a bright white light falling like a meteor toward the Earth.

He expected it to burn out quickly, long before it hit the ground, but it kept getting larger and brighter and closer. His eyes widened in alarm.

"It's heading for the farm!" he exclaimed. "Our farm!"

The Kents had farmed this land for five generations. Jonathan's heart pounded as he hit the gas and raced their dusty pickup truck at top speed toward their land. He and Martha exchanged worried looks.

"What if it hits the house?" she asked. "Or the barn?"

"I don't know," he said grimly.

The Kent family farm came into view. Moonlight exposed the farmhouse, a large red barn, and a grain silo. A tall wooden windmill towered over the farm, while acres of freshly grown corn and wheat waited to be harvested. The meteor came whistling down from the night sky like a missile, trailing fire behind it.

"Watch out!" Jonathan said. "Here it comes!"

The meteor hit the cornfields with earth-shaking force, throwing up a huge cloud of dust and dirt. The road shook, and Jonathan struggled to keep control of the truck, which veered wildly across the road.

The vehicle almost hit a telephone pole, but Jonathan managed to steer it back onto the road. He slammed on the brakes, and the pickup squealed to a halt. He and Martha scrambled out of the truck, gasping for breath. Wide-eyed, they stared in shock at the billowing cloud above the field. Thick rows of cornstalks blocked their view of the crash site.

"What—what was that?" Martha asked.

"Let's go see," Jonathan said.

The dust cloud began to settle. Jonathan was glad that the meteor had missed their house. He hoped that not too many crops had been ruined, but then he saw something that worried him even more.

Smoke was rising up from the field, right where the meteorite (or whatever it was) had crashed. He smelled something burning.

"The crops!" he exclaimed. "They're on fire!"

The Smallville fire station was miles away. There was no time to run to the house and dial 911. They had to put out the fire quickly, before it wiped out a year's worth of crops. Jonathan grabbed a heavy-duty tarp from the back of the truck. He and Martha ran into the fields, following the smell of smoke. Their hearts were racing.

"Hurry!" Jonathan called. "Maybe we can still put it out before it spreads!"

Martha chased after him as they ran through rows of cornstalks. She worried about being caught in the middle of the fire with no way out. What if the whole field exploded into flame?

"Be careful!" she shouted. "That corn isn't worth our lives!"

They burst through the rows to find an astounding sight. What they had seen streaming through the sky hadn't been a meteor at all. A large space capsule, roughly the size of a tractor, was lying at the bottom of a newly carved crater in the middle of the field. A carpet of flattened cornstalks had been set on fire by the UFO's crash landing. Jonathan knew at once that the steaming object was no ordinary meteorite, but he and Martha needed to deal with the fire first. Their livelihoods depended on it. If they lost the crops, they could lose the farm.

"Wait!" Martha said. "Do you hear that?"

At first, all Jonathan heard was the crackle of the flames, but then he heard something else. Something completely unexpected.

A baby crying.

"Good heavens!" she said. "It's coming from inside that thing!"

Jonathan blinked in surprise.

A baby?

"It's in danger, Jonathan," she exclaimed. "We have to save it!"

"I know," Jonathan said.

Now, more than ever, they had to put out the fire. They hurried down the steep sides of the crater, sliding awkwardly on the loose soil. On the bright side, the walls of the crater were keeping the flames from spreading too quickly, but their worries about the corn, and their own safety, took second place to saving the baby inside the space capsule. Jonathan used the heavy tarp to beat down the larger flames, while Martha fought the smaller fires with her jacket. They couldn't let a single spark escape or the entire field could be set ablaze.

The heat from the flames was intense and scary. The smoke stung their eyes. Sweat dripped from Jonathan and Martha's faces as they frantically fought the fire until every last spark and ember was extinguished. Soot covered their faces, and they were breathing hard. The air smelled like popcorn. Jonathan ground a stubborn red ember beneath the heel of his boot.

"That's it, I think," Jonathan said, panting. He glanced around to see if they had missed anything, but all he saw was ashes. His aching arms let go of the heavy tarp, which was badly singed around the edges. "The fire's out."

"Thank heavens!" Martha said. "But what about the baby?"

Jonathan had not forgotten about the baby. He could still hear it wailing inside the crashed space capsule. Now that the fire was extinguished, it was finally safe to inspect the UFO—and find out who was crying.

"Who drops a baby out of the sky?" Martha asked aloud.

"I wish I knew," Jonathan said.

They cautiously approached the UFO. A curved hatchway, blackened by the heat, slid open and revealed a padded cavity inside the space capsule. A healthy-looking baby was tucked inside, crying his lungs out. To their surprise, the infant appeared unharmed by the fire or the crash. He wasn't burned at all.

"Oh, the poor thing!"

Martha rushed forward to rescue the infant. She lifted the baby from the capsule and gently cradled him in her arms. Comforted, the baby stopped crying. He gazed up at Jonathan and Martha with wide blue eyes. A tuft of black hair clung to his scalp.

"Where—where do you think he came from?" Martha asked.

Jonathan examined the space capsule from a safe distance. It didn't look like anything he had ever seen, except maybe in a science fiction movie. There was something almost biological about it, as though it had been *grown* instead of constructed. Overlapping plates, made of hardened bone or shell, protected the exterior of the spacecraft. The padding inside the cavity looked like some kind of silk. A sticky layer of gel coated the silk.

"I don't know," he said. "Maybe the Russians?"

Martha shook her head. "Look at that ship, Jonathan. Does that look like it came from anywhere on Earth?"

"Not really." He lifted his eyes to stare at the stars. "You think he came from . . . somewhere else?"

He inspected the baby in his wife's arms. The infant looked perfectly human, but was he really a strange visitor from another planet? Jonathan had never given much thought to the subject of aliens and UFOs before. It

31

was hard to imagine that one had just landed in his field.

But where else could the baby have come from?

"I suppose we should notify the authorities," he said.

"No!" Martha said with surprising force. "We can't turn this poor baby over to the government. Who knows what they'll do to him, especially if they think he's some sort of alien invader. They might lock him up in a laboratory somewhere . . . or worse." She held on tightly to the child. "Look at him, Jonathan! He's just a baby. He needs somebody to take care of him, someone who will love him no matter where he came from."

"Like us?" Jonathan asked.

They had always wanted a child of their own, but things had not worked out that way. Now, it seemed, a baby had literally dropped out of the sky.

"Why not?" she asked.

"But we can't adopt a baby just like that," he objected. "That's not how it's normally done. There are rules and regulations about this sort of thing. You can't just adopt a baby like it's a stray kitten you found under the porch."

She nodded at the alien space capsule.

"Nothing about this situation is normal, Jonathan. I don't think the usual rules apply when it comes to babies from outer space."

He could tell her mind was made up. To be honest, he didn't like the idea of turning the baby over to the government any more than she did. The arrival of a being from another planet could scare a lot of people, and scared people sometimes did bad things out of fear. They might see this innocent baby as a monster that needed to be locked up or even destroyed. Or scientists might want to perform inhumane tests and experiments on him.

Jonathan wasn't going to allow that.

"Well, what do we want to call him anyway?"

"I was thinking Clark." She smiled down at the gurgling baby, who looked very content in her arms. "Clark Kent."

CHAPTER THREE

"He won't stop crying," Martha told the doctor.

The unhappy baby was sitting on an examining table in Dr. Whitaker's office, while his adoptive parents looked on anxiously. Jonathan and Martha had been reluctant to take little Clark to see the doctor in the first place, for fear that a thorough examination would reveal the baby's unusual origins, but Clark's constant crying had left them no choice.

It wasn't just that they couldn't get any sleep. They

were also worried that something might be seriously wrong with Clark. What did they know about taking care of an alien baby? At times, Clark seemed to have trouble breathing, as though he were struggling to adapt to Earth's atmosphere. That seemed to be getting better slowly, but what if his crying jags were a symptom of a deeper problem? They had no idea what they were dealing with.

"It's probably just colic," Dr. Whitaker said. The gray-haired pediatrician was a fixture in Smallville who had treated several generations of kids. He peered at Clark through a thick pair of glasses. "Some babies are just more sensitive to sights and sounds than others. It upsets them until they get used to it."

He brought out a machine to measure Clark's hearing. He placed the tip of an earplug into the baby's ear. A cord connected the plug to the measuring device.

"Don't worry," he told the anxious parents. "The test is completely painless."

Jonathan and Martha exchanged worried looks.

They had no idea how Clark might react to the test—or what could happen if it scared him. Clark wasn't like other children. They knew that already.

"I'm not sure that's a good idea," Jonathan began. "Maybe we—"

The doctor was used to nervous parents. "Don't worry," he insisted. "It's a routine procedure."

He flipped a switch on the device.

Clark's wails went up in volume—to a superhuman degree. He shrieked loud enough to break every window in the office. In the clinic's waiting room, a gumball machine shattered, spilling candy onto the carpet. An aquarium burst, flooding the waiting room. Alarms went off outside as car windshields and storefront windows cracked all along Main Street. Dr. Whitaker's glasses cracked as well. He blinked in surprise behind the broken lenses.

"What in the world—?"

Jonathan darted forward and plucked the plug from Clark's ear. The baby stopped crying as Martha rescued him from the examining table.

The Kents decided that now was a good time to leave. Dr. Whitaker was too dazed to protest as they hurried out of the office. Martha winced at the mess in the waiting room, where the receptionist was too busy rescuing the fish from the aquarium to notice the Kents leaving. More broken glass and confusion waited for them on the street outside. Windows were broken everywhere, and even the traffic lights were cracked. People were shouting and scratching their heads. Baby Clark giggled at the commotion, while his parents shook their heads in dismay. They walked quickly back toward their truck.

"I knew this was a mistake," Jonathan muttered.

"I guess so," Martha agreed. She hoped that the damage would be blamed on a freak natural disturbance, like perhaps an earthquake or sonic boom, instead of a single baby crying. That would sound more believable to most people. It certainly sounded more believable to her.

But they had learned a valuable lesson.

No more doctors for Clark.

"Where did you find this again?"

The scientist handed the sample back to Jonathan. It was a small piece of the mysterious space capsule that Jonathan had managed to pry loose from the hull. Only the fact that one of the outer heat panels had been partially dislodged by the capsule's fiery crash landing had allowed Jonathan to break off a tiny black flake that was barely more than an inch long. He had driven all the way to Kansas State University to have the fragment examined by a trained metallurgist. It was a risk showing the sample to anyone outside the family, but after what had happened at the doctor's office, Jonathan was desperate to find out *something* about where Clark had come from.

"I'm sorry. I can't tell you that," Jonathan said. "It's personal."

"I was afraid of that," Professor Metcalfe said. He

was about the same age as Jonathan. He eyed the fragment enviously, clearly reluctant to give it up. "That sample is like nothing I've ever seen before. I ran every test I could think of and I still can't identify it. There are elements in that compound that aren't even on the periodic table!"

Jonathan was a farmer, not a scientist, but he knew what a big deal that was. The periodic table was a chart listing every element known to modern science. He remembered that from high school chemistry.

"Could it have come from some place . . . not of this world?"

"Like an asteroid or meteorite?" the professor said. "Possibly. There's certainly nothing earthly about it."

Jonathan nodded. The scientist was only confirming what he and Martha had always suspected. Clark was from another planet, no matter how human he looked. He was never going to be a normal boy.

"Are you sure I can't show the sample to some of my colleagues?" Metcalfe asked. "I can think of plenty of scientists, all over the world, who would love to get a look at this."

Jonathan knew that the scientist had to be dying of curiosity. He felt bad about disappointing him, but Clark's safety came first. There was no way of knowing how the world would react to the news that an alien was growing up in Smallville. They needed to keep Clark off the radar until he was old enough to make his own decision about whether or not to reveal himself to the world.

"Right now I need you to forget about this," he said firmly. "I'm sorry. I know it's a lot to ask, but—"

"What are friends for," Bill Metcalfe said. He and Jonathan had played football together in Smallville many years ago. Jonathan had even saved Bill's life once when he'd fallen through the ice on a frozen river. "I'll keep quiet for old time's sake."

Jonathan trusted Metcalfe to keep his promise. He tucked the sample securely away in his pocket. The rest of the space capsule was already hidden in an old barn on the farm. John had used a tractor to drag the capsule out of the fields and had later filled in the crater created by the crash. It had been a big job, but all evidence of Clark's spectacular arrival had been covered up. Jonathan hoped that would be enough.

"You'll destroy the lab reports?" he asked.

"If you insist." The scientist shrugged. "Probably just as well. Nobody would believe the results anyway!"

CHAPTER FOUR

Three years later . . .

"Clark, honey. Put down your blocks. We have company."

Martha stood on the front porch, watching nervously as the visitors' station wagon approached the farm. It was a clear spring day, but a sudden chill ran down her spine. She wondered if it was too late to call off this playdate.

Maybe this was a bad idea.

On the other hand, they couldn't hide Clark from the neighbors forever. He deserved a chance to play with children his own age, so she had invited Sarah Lang to drop by for a visit. Sarah's little daughter, Lana, was only a few months younger than Clark, who had just celebrated his third birthday.

Not that they actually knew what Clark's real birthday was, of course, or even where he had been born. She and Jonathan had simply chosen the date of the space capsule's arrival as his birthday. Clark didn't know any better—and neither did anybody else. Martha wanted to keep it that way.

"Did you hear me, Clark? Put down your blocks."

The toddler, who had thoroughly adapted to Earth's atmosphere by now, was already playing in the yard. His "blocks" were actually five-pound bricks that Clark stacked as easily as if they were made of wood or plastic. He preferred them to regular blocks, which he could crush if he squeezed them too hard. Despite his age, Clark was already stronger and faster than most adults. Martha and Jonathan were trying to teach him to control his strength, especially around other people, but he was still learning.

What if he slipped up in front of Sarah?

Jonathan was working in the fields. He had argued against this experiment, but Martha had insisted—for Clark's sake. She wanted Clark to have friends, like any other child.

The station wagon pulled up to the house and parked in the driveway. Forgetting about his blocks, Clark ran to greet their visitors. Martha put on a happy face and hoped for the best. It was too late to turn back now.

"Hi, Sarah," she called out as the Langs got out of the car. She waved at the visitors. "Glad you could make it!"

"Thanks for inviting us," Sarah said. She noticed the piles of bricks stacked randomly around the yard. "Is Jonathan building something?"

"An art project . . . or maybe a barbecue pit. I'm not sure."

"Oh," Sarah said, sounding slightly puzzled.

Lana was a sweet little girl with red curls, who didn't seem shy at all. For a moment, Martha envied Sarah for having a perfectly human child, but then she caught herself. Clark was her son. She wouldn't trade him for anything.

"Clark, this is Lana," Martha said. "Say hello."

"Hello, Lana."

"Hi, Clark," the other child replied. "Want to play?"

"You bet!" Clark grinned, obviously thrilled to have a playmate at last. He took off across the lawn. "Try to catch me!"

"Not too rough!" Martha called out. "Play nice!"

"Don't worry," Sarah said. "A little horseplay never hurt anyone."

Easy for you to say, Martha thought.

The moms settled down on the porch to have iced tea while the children played happily in the yard. After a while, Martha began to relax. So far everything was going smoothly. She was glad that the children were getting along. It would be good for Clark to have friends, despite his secret.

"So, have you heard the news from town?" Sarah said, eager to share the latest gossip with Martha. "They say that the mayor and the police chief are barely speaking to each other. . . ."

Martha wasn't very interested in local politics, but pretended to pay attention. She sipped her tea while keeping a close eye on the kids—and nearly choked on the drink when she saw Clark pick Lana up and toss her straight into the air!

Squealing happily, the little girl shot up to at least fifteen feet above the ground before dropping back into little Clark's arms. Martha gasped in relief as he caught her gently, but then he threw her up in the air again. This time she rose higher than the house.

Clark ran to catch her.

"Whee!" Lana said. "I'm flying!"

Martha's heart skipped a beat, although Sarah was too busy trading gossip to notice what was happening in the yard. Martha jumped up from her chair and moved hastily to block the other woman's view. She couldn't let Sarah see this. There was no way she could explain how strong Clark was!

"Sarah!" she said urgently. "I think I left some ice cream out on the kitchen counter. Would you be a dear and run inside to check? I'll keep an eye on the kids."

"No problem," Sarah said with a shrug. She tried to peer around Martha, who casually shifted position to keep Sarah from seeing what exactly Lana was squealing about. It sounded like the kids were just having a fun time together.

"Please, hurry!" Martha said. "I don't want it to melt all over the place."

Sarah scurried inside and Martha rushed down into the yard. Clark was just catching Lana again when she caught up with the kids. She breathed a sigh of relief as she saw that Lana seemed to be perfectly fine.

"Clark! Lana! That's enough of that game for now. Why don't you come up on the porch with us? We can have ice cream!"

That was enough to distract the kids from their new game, but Martha was a nervous wreck the whole time they were eating dessert on the porch. She forced herself to keep smiling even while she worried. What if Sarah had seen what Clark could do? What if Lana had been hurt—or worse?

Jonathan was right, she realized. This was a bad idea.

"I'm sorry," she said finally. "I'm afraid I have a splitting headache. Will you forgive me if we cut this visit short? I think I need to lie down."

She didn't really have a headache. She just wanted to send Sarah and Lana home before something else happened.

"Of course," Sarah said. "Come along, Lana. It's time to go."

The children said good-bye to each other. Martha thanked Sarah for understanding.

"We'll have to do this again sometime," she lied.

Martha knew better now. They couldn't let Clark play with other children. It was too dangerous—for everyone. Clark would be lonely and disappointed, but there was no way around it. He was different from other children. She couldn't risk anyone finding out the truth about him. She couldn't bear it if the government came and took him away.

Poor Clark, she thought. He had looked so happy to have a friend.

Maybe they could get him a dog?

CHAPTER FIVE

Three years later . . .

Clark stared up at the fluffy white clouds drifting
over his parents' farm. It was a bright spring day, and
the warm afternoon sun filled him with energy. Now a
healthy, active six-year-old, Clark was fascinated by the
sky. He often watched hawks circling high above the farm
and wondered what it would be like to fly among them.
The tempting clouds were too far away. He wanted to

reach out and touch them.

A breeze turned the blades of the windmill, way up high. An idea occurred to Clark, and he scampered over to the base of the towering wooden structure. His dad was busy puttering with the tractor over by the barn, and his mom was potting geraniums on the front porch, so neither of them noticed when Clark started climbing the windmill.

He grinned in excitement.

A wooden ladder led up the side of the windmill. His little arms and legs were just long enough to reach the rungs, and he quickly reached the top, dozens of feet above the ground. Although the drifting clouds were still too far away to reach, the breathtaking view was worth the climb. He could see all the way to Smallville and beyond. Acres of rolling fields and farmland stretched out as far as the eye could see. The nearest farm was miles away and looked like a dollhouse from this height. Golden sunlight warmed Clark's face. He couldn't get enough of it.

"Clark!"

His mom's frightened voice startled Clark. She dropped a flower pot, which shattered loudly on the porch. She stared up at him with a terrified expression and placed a hand over her heart. Alerted by her cry, Jonathan dropped what he was doing as well and ran toward the windmill. He looked scared to death.

"Don't move, Clark!" he shouted anxiously. "Stay right where you are!"

Clark gulped. He hadn't been scared before, but his parents' panicked reactions reminded him just how high up he was—and how far he could fall. He peered down at the ground too many feet below. The windmill seemed much higher than it had from the ground. It was a very long way down.

If he slipped and fell . . .

"I'm coming, Clark!" Jonathan yelled. "Be careful! Don't move!"

His father's shouts hurt Clark's ears. All of a sudden, everything was too loud, as though somebody had turned up the volume on the entire world. The turning blades of the windmill sounded like a jet engine. He could hear his own heart pounding like a jackhammer, and he heard his parents' heartbeats even from far away. A gentle breeze roared like a hurricane. A squawking bird sounded like a dinosaur. He clapped one hand over an ear, trying to keep out the deafening noise, but it was no good. He could hear *everything*.

And there was something wrong with his eyes, too. Staring down at the ground, he saw *through* the dirt and gravel to the bedrock underneath. He spied an underground stream trickling beneath the well, as well as a buried septic tank in the backyard. Lights and colors shifted before his eyes, making him sick to his stomach. The reds were way too red. The purples got darker and more intense. Lifting his gaze, he saw that the sturdy wooden walls of his house now looked as clear as glass, so that he could see the rooms and furniture inside, as well as the pipes and wires inside the walls. The barns and grain silo also turned transparent. It was like his eyes were X-ray machines, running out of control.

He started to cry.

"Clark!" his mom called out. "Don't be scared, honey! It will be okay!"

Clark looked to her for comfort, only to shriek in fright. His mom's skin and muscles and clothes had disappeared so that all he saw were her bones. She looked like a living skeleton, hurrying toward the windmill. Petrified by the ghastly sight, he glanced down at his dad—and saw another skeleton climbing toward him. A fleshless skull looked up at him. Empty eye sockets peered at Clark.

"What is it, son?" the skull said with his father's voice. "What's the matter?"

Startled, Clark lost his balance. He slipped and fell off the windmill, plunging toward the ground below. The wind whipped past his face as he screamed in terror. Although he was only a little kid, he knew that a fall like this could break every bone in his body— and probably even kill him.

He heard his mother screaming, too.

It sounded like a police siren.

Clark hit the ground hard, landing face-first in the dirt. The impact knocked the breath out of him, but after a moment, he was surprised to find himself alive and in one piece. At first, he was afraid to move. He cautiously tested his arms and legs, half-expecting them not to work anymore. But they weren't broken or even sore. He rolled over and touched his face.

He wasn't even bleeding.

"Clark!" His mom ran to his side and looked him over frantically. She seemed as surprised as he was at how unharmed he was. "Oh my goodness, are you all right?"

"I . . . I think so."

He stood up carefully and brushed the dirt and gravel from his clothes. His crash landing had left a Clark-shaped impression in the ground, six inches deep, but he was already feeling better. His mother's pounding heartbeat faded away. Her skin materialized back over her bones so that she looked like his mom again.

Jonathan dropped to the ground and hurried to join them. He wasn't a skeleton anymore either. His face was no longer a skull. The colors around Clark went back to normal, while the walls of the house turned solid again. The world got less noisy. His ears stopped aching.

"Is he hurt?" Jonathan said as he knelt down beside Clark. His worried eyes were better than empty sockets. "Do we need to call an ambulance?"

Martha shook her head. She looked both relieved and worried at the same time. She hugged Clark, gently at first, but more tightly once she was sure he wasn't broken inside. He hugged her back, carefully. He didn't want to break her.

"I think he's fine, Jonathan. The fall . . . it didn't hurt him at all."

"But—?"

Jonathan started to say something, but changed his mind. He just nodded at Martha and checked Clark out for himself. He held up two fingers. "How many fingers do you see?"

They were normal fingers, not skeleton fingers.

"Two," Clark said.

His dad nodded, satisfied that Clark didn't have a concussion. He scratched his head in bewilderment and then shrugged his shoulders.

"I'm just glad you're okay, son."

Clark didn't understand. What had just happened to his eyes and ears—and why hadn't the fall hurt him? He gazed up at the windmill, which was as high as the grain silo. He had fallen all the way from the top. He should be broken to pieces, like Humpty Dumpty.

"But why am I okay?" he said. "It doesn't make any sense."

His parents exchanged a tense look. Clark sensed that there was something they didn't want to talk about in front of him—like it was a grown-up secret or something. He wished they would tell him what was going on.

"Let's just call it a miracle," his mom said.

"For now," Jonathan muttered under his breath.

"So I don't need to see a doctor?" Clark asked. He

had never actually been to a doctor before, that he could remember. His mom and dad had always said it wasn't necessary, since he never got sick. It occurred to Clark that he had never hurt himself like the kids he saw on TV. He had never skinned his knee or busted his lip or gotten a black eye or bruises. He'd never even had a toothache or a cavity.

"Nope," his dad said. "You lucked out, buster. In fact, I think it might be a good idea if you didn't mention this to anyone. Let's keep it our secret."

"How come?" Clark asked.

His parents gave each other funny looks again. Jonathan sighed, the way he did whenever he needed to have an Important Talk with Clark. The boy hoped he wasn't in too much trouble for climbing the windmill. He hadn't meant to scare his parents like that.

But his dad didn't seem worried about that right now. He had other things on his mind.

"Because . . . people might not understand, son."

Clark was confused. "Understand what?"

His father struggled to find the right words. "The way you fell so far and didn't get hurt, some people might be . . . confused . . . by that. It might even scare them."

"But why?" Clark asked, getting more and more concerned. He felt like he had done something wrong, but he didn't know what. "Was it a bad thing that I didn't get hurt?"

"No, of course not!" his mother insisted. She dabbed a tear from her eye. "You have no idea how relieved I am right now. For a few moments there . . ."

She couldn't finish the sentence.

"This *was* a miracle, Clark," his dad insisted. "But it could make people think that you're . . . different . . . from other children. And that might upset them."

Clark's throat tightened. "Am I different?"

His father took a deep breath before answering. "You're *special*, Clark. Very special in ways we don't even know yet. But we can't let anybody know that, at least not right now." He placed a hand on Clark's shoulder and looked sternly into the boy's eyes. "I'm serious about this, Clark. Do you understand me?"

Clark nodded. "But why am I different?"

"*Special*," Jonathan repeated. "And I can't really explain that right now. You'll understand when you're older."

"But I want to know now!"

His father shook his head. "When you're older," he promised. "But, for now, this *has* to be a secret, just between the three of us. Promise me you won't tell anybody about this."

"I promise," Clark said, although he didn't understand why. "Cross my heart."

His dad nodded and stood up. He glanced over at the windmill.

"Now then," he said, "what on earth were you thinking, Clark? Climbing all the way up there? Do you know how much you scared your mother and me?"

Clark felt bad about that. He knew he was in hot water, but he tried to explain. He hoped his folks would go easy on him.

"I just wanted to touch the sky," he said.

CHAPTER SIX

Four years later . . .

Shelby was Clark's best friend. To be honest, he was just about Clark's only friend. The scruffy brown terrier was running around the front yard, his tail wagging enthusiastically. He and Clark were playing fetch after school, a game the energetic puppy couldn't get enough of. Shelby barked happily as Clark hurled a stick into the air.

"Go get it!" Clark said.

The dog chased after the stick. He jumped and caught it in midair.

"Good catch, Shelby!" Clark said. "Attaboy!"

The dog trotted back to Clark, carrying the stick in his jaws. Clark knew Shelby wanted him to throw the stick again, but first they had to play a bit of tug-of-war. Clark grabbed part of the stick and pretended that he couldn't yank it from the dog's mouth. Clark had to watch his strength. He was ten years old now and getting stronger every day—and faster, too.

"C'mon, boy. Let it go." They pulled back and forth on the stick. Shelby shook his head, refusing to surrender. Clark played along. "Ooh, you're too strong for me, you tough little dog! Give it to me. Come on, let go."

Shelby held on to the stick for a few more minutes before getting bored with the game. He released the stick, which now had dog drool all over it. Clark tried not to touch the slimy parts, but that was easier said than done. He wiped his gooey fingers off on his jeans.

"Ick," he muttered.

A pickup truck turned into the driveway and pulled up to the house. Jonathan Kent got out of the truck, carrying a bag of groceries he had picked up in town. He smiled at Clark and Shelby playing in the yard. It had been a good idea to get Clark a dog to keep him company. The boy deserved one friend at least.

"Looks like you and Shelby are having fun," Jonathan said. He headed for the front porch. "Let me run these groceries in to your mom and maybe I'll join you."

"Hey, Dad," Clark said. "Wait up."

Despite the dog yapping at his heels, wanting to play some more, Clark hurried toward his dad. He had been waiting for a chance like this, while working up his nerve. Now seemed like a good time.

"You have a minute?"

"Sure, son." He put down the groceries on the front step. "What's up?"

Clark took a deep breath. He had been rehearsing

this conversation in his head all day. He wanted it to go well.

"I was just wondering," he began, "if you'd had a chance to think some more about what we were talking about before. You know, about me joining a soccer team . . . like the other kids."

His father sighed.

"Clark, I thought we settled this. I don't think it's a good idea."

"But it's not fair," Clark said. "Everybody else gets to play sports. They're having sign-ups this weekend. It's not too late!"

"But you're *not* everybody, Clark. You know that. What if you get caught up in the game and accidentally reveal how strong and fast you *really* are? Or, even worse, what if you hurt somebody by mistake?"

"I'll be really careful!" Clark promised. "You can trust me!"

"I do trust you, Clark. I know you'd do your best. But it's not worth the risk."

The planet Krypton is doomed. Jor-El and Lara save their only son by sending him to Earth.

The Kryptonian shuttle lands near a farmhouse in Kansas. Jonathan and Martha Kent adopt the baby, naming him Clark.

Clark and Jonathan share a special bond.

Even from a young age, Clark knows he is different.
What he does not know is that he is destined to do great things.

Clark's classmates bully him relentlessly. Luckily, his father is around to protect him.

Jonathan reveals the truth behind Clark's amazing abilities.

Clark embraces his special powers and uses them to protect others as Superman—the Man of Steel!

"Easy for you to say," Clark said. "You're not the one stuck playing with a dumb dog all the time." He glanced down at Shelby, who was still bouncing around his feet, waiting impatiently for Clark to throw the stick again. The boy felt a twinge of guilt. It wasn't Shelby's fault that his parents wouldn't let him take part in sports. He patted the dog on the head. "Sorry, boy. I didn't mean that."

"Look, I understand," Dad said. "I know this is hard on you, and I wish it didn't have to be this way, but right now we need to play it safe. Maybe someday, when you're older—"

"You always say that!" Clark felt like he had been hearing the same lecture for his entire life, probably because he had been. He was sick and tired of hearing it. He wanted more. "How long do I have to keep hiding what I can do?"

"I don't know, son." His dad picked up the groceries and headed indoors. He paused in the doorway to look back at Clark. "I'm sorry, but this decision is final."

The front door swung shut behind him, leaving Clark and Shelby alone in the front yard. The puppy was still barking frantically to get the boy's attention. Clark felt like the whole world was ganging up on him. Why did his dad have to be so stubborn all the time? Why couldn't he listen for once?

"All right, all right," Clark said impatiently. "Here! Go get it!"

Frustrated, he flung the stick with all his strength. It flew from his hand and he realized, a second too late, that he had thrown it too hard. The stick flew through the air, heading straight for the attic window.

"Oh, no!" Clark said. "Not now!"

He panicked as he imagined the runaway stick smashing through the window, right after he'd told his father that he could control his own strength. If Clark broke the window now, it would be proof that his father had been right all along.

His dad would never ease up on him!

Desperate to catch the spinning stick before it hit the

window, Clark leapt into the air after it. His powerful legs carried him three stories high and he reached desperately for the stick. His outstretched fingers caught hold of the stick, which was still slippery with dog drool. It almost got away from him, but he managed to snag onto it at the last minute. He gasped in relief.

"Got you!"

But who had *him*?

Momentum kept him flying upward, unable to stop himself. Instead of the stick, it was Clark who smashed through the window—and kept on going. He flew through the attic roof like a cannonball and blasted through the chimney, too. Solid bricks shattered and rained down from the roof, along with broken glass, wood, and shingles. The crash was loud enough to be heard all across the farm. Shelby barked wildly at the commotion.

Oh boy, Clark thought, *I'm in trouble now.*

He tried to grab onto something to halt his flight, but everything was happening too fast. He shot past the roof into the sky and arced high above the farm before gravity finally caught up with him. Falling from the sky, he crashed down into a haystack out past the barn. Loose straw was thrown up into the air. Alarmed chickens sought shelter in their coop.

He wasn't surprised that the fall hadn't hurt him, but that wasn't what he was worried about. He could already hear his parents shouting in the front yard, while Shelby barked up a storm. Clark scrambled out of the haystack, straw clinging to his hair and clothes. He brushed slivers of broken glass from his arms and legs, not concerned about getting cut. His red flannel shirt was torn and shredded in places. He nervously checked out the damage to the farmhouse.

He couldn't see the front of the house from here, but the chimney was a total loss. It was smashed to pieces. All that was left was a pile of shattered bricks strewn across the wounded rooftop. Clark gulped. He didn't even want to look at the rest of the house.

"Clark!" his dad called angrily. "Get over here!"

For a second, Clark considered running away. If he started running now, he could be in another county in minutes. He could be in another *state* before his parents realized he was gone.

But they had raised him better than that.

Clark knew he had to face the music, so he ran back to the yard, not quite as quickly as possible. The wind from his speed blew the last bits of straw and glass from his clothes.

"Here I am," he said. "I'm sorry."

His parents were both out in the front yard, staring up at the damage. There was a gaping hole where the attic window used to be, and another hole in the roof beyond. Broken glass and bricks littered the porch roof. It looked like a missile had struck the house—which was pretty much the case.

Except the missile was Clark.

Shelby barked at Clark, who realized, sheepishly, that he was still holding onto the stick. He gave it to the dog to play with.

"Oh, Clark," his mother said. She sounded more disappointed than angry. She shook her head sadly. "You need to be more careful."

"I can fix it!" Clark said hastily. "You know I can. It won't cost a thing."

He wasn't fooling. With his strength and speed, he was sure he could repair the roof faster than humanly possible, as long as his dad showed him what to do, that is. All he needed was a hammer and some nails, and some fresh wood and bricks. He wondered how much the raw materials would cost.

Maybe they could take it out of his allowance?

"That's not the point, Clark," his dad said. He pointed at the wrecked attic and window. "This is just what we were talking about. Suppose somebody had seen you—or gotten hurt because of your carelessness?"

Clark didn't know what to say. He stared at his feet.

"But . . . I didn't mean to. It was an accident."

"I know," his father said sternly. "But I want you to

remember this. Do you understand now? *This* is why you can't play soccer with the other kids."

Clark looked up at the wreckage. He knew his dad was right.

But that didn't make him feel any better.

CHAPTER SEVEN

Four months later . . .

"Clark! You're going to miss your bus!"

His mother's voice reached Clark in the backyard,
where he had been using his heat vision to melt the snow
off the back porch. Bright red beams shot from his eyes,
turning the packed snow and ice to steam. Clark had
figured out how to fire heat rays from his eyes years ago,
when he had accidentally set a comic book on fire while
learning how to read. He didn't know why he could do

such a freaky thing, but all he had to do was focus on something and . . . concentrate.

It was easier than shoveling.

"Oh, no!" he exclaimed. Caught up in his chores, he had lost track of the time. A horn honked in the distance. He looked toward the road at the end of the long driveway and saw the yellow school bus arriving. He raced toward the road, but slipped on a patch of ice.

Oops!

The fall didn't—couldn't—hurt him. But by the time he scrambled to his feet, the bus had already pulled away. Whitney Fordham, a mean kid from school, made faces at Clark through the bus's back window. He stuck out his tongue.

"Wait!" Clark shouted. "Wait for me!"

The bus didn't stop or turn around. Clark guessed that the bus driver hadn't seen him, perhaps because he was concentrating on the icy road. Or maybe the driver was just on a tight schedule and didn't feel like giving a late arrival a break. For whatever reason, the bus left Clark behind.

"Shoot," he said, angrily kicking the snow at the curb. He vaporized the inconvenient patch of ice with a red-hot blast of heat vision.

It didn't help.

Clark didn't know what to do. He couldn't be late for school. There was a big test in social studies that morning. He looked back at the farm, but his dad had already left with the truck an hour ago to pick up supplies in town. Clark wasn't sure when he was due back. Not before school started, probably.

Clark was on his own.

There was only one thing to do. Clark looked up and down the road to make sure no one was watching and then took off running. Cutting across snow-covered fields, he sprinted toward town faster than any bus. His super-speed melted the snow, obscuring his tracks. Steam rose behind him. Anyone watching would have seen only a blur of motion.

Clark grinned as he ran. It felt good to cut loose for once.

He slowed down as he neared the school, arriving only a few moments before the bus did. Whitney gaped in surprise when he saw Clark strolling up the sidewalk outside the school. The bully scowled as he got off the bus. He was a head taller than Clark, who was small for his age. He caught up with Clark.

"Hey!" he said. "How'd you get here so fast, Kent?"

Clark shrugged. "Took a shortcut."

He started to walk away, but Whitney grabbed his shoulder. "Not so fast," the bully growled. "I'm talking to you, Kent!"

Clark's heart sank. Whitney had been picking on him since second grade. He was sick and tired of it. Times like this he almost wished that his parents had homeschooled him like his dad had wanted to. Clark's mom had convinced his father to let him go to the school like any other kid. Clark had been grateful, even though it meant dealing with bullies like Whitney.

"Just leave me alone, Whitney."

"Oh, yeah?" The bully shoved Clark so hard that he stumbled forward, spilling his books and homework onto the sidewalk. An American history textbook landed in puddle of melted ice and slush. Whitney barked harshly. "Make me!"

Clark wished he could. Not for the first time, he was tempted to show Whitney what he could really do. Solar fire hid behind Clark's eyes. He clenched his fists. If he wanted to, he could send Whitney flying across the sidewalk—and beyond.

But it wasn't worth it.

He had promised his parents that he wouldn't reveal what he could do. And, now that he was older, he understood why it was so important. He didn't want people to think he was different either. He just wanted to be treated like a normal kid, not a freak who shot laser beams from his eyes. Or who could outrace a school bus.

So, instead of throwing Whitney all the way across

town, or giving him a hotfoot he would never forget, Clark just gathered up his books and tried to walk away. His history book was soaking wet. He hoped it wasn't ruined.

"That's enough, Whitney," Lana Lang scolded him. She and Clark were still neighbors, although he didn't know her well because he had to keep to himself. His mom said that they had once played together as kids, although Clark barely remembered that. She got between Whitney and Clark. "Why don't you pick on somebody your own size?"

Clark cringed. He appreciated Lana sticking up for him, but it was embarrassing not to be able to stand up for himself. His cheeks burned as he heard the other kids laughing at him. This kept getting worse and worse.

"It's okay, Lana," he lied. "It's no big deal."

A warning bell rang. Clark hurried toward his first class.

"That's right, Kent," Whitney taunted him. "Run away . . . just like you always do!"

One of these days, Clark thought. *Just you wait . . .*

He was still fuming inside when he sat down in class to take Mr. Plummer's social studies test. Clark had already read the entire textbook at super-speed, so he finished the test way before the other students. With time to kill, he amused himself by playing with his X-ray vision. He had learned to control his vision years ago, so he had fun by turning the teacher and his classmates into human skeletons or anatomy lessons. He could look beneath their skin to see the muscles and organs underneath. Hearts pumped inside bony rib cages. Lungs inflated with air. He could even look into people's stomachs to see what they'd had for breakfast. Mr. Plummer seemed to like scrambled eggs and bacon.

It was gross, but in a cool way, and it was good practice when it came to mastering his special abilities.

Maybe I should be a doctor when I grow up, Clark thought. *I wouldn't even need an X-ray machine to see what was wrong with my patients.*

When peeking inside people got boring, he turned

his telescopic vision toward the town outside. He could watch all of Smallville from the classroom and even look through the walls of the buildings. He didn't spy on private homes or offices, because that would be bad manners, but there was no reason he couldn't watch one of the movies playing at the Smallville Cinema several blocks away. If he concentrated, he could even hear all the dialogue and music. He enjoyed a bit of a new science fiction movie from his desk at school. It was a pretty good film, all about a visitor from another planet. Clark liked that he could entertain himself this way without anyone knowing. It beat watching the clock while the other kids worked on the test.

Sometimes there were advantages to being different.

"Clark? Are you done with your test?"

His teacher's voice dragged Clark away from the movie. Letting his vision switch back to normal, Clark saw that the class was over. The other students were all turning in their tests and heading to their next classes.

"Sorry," Clark said. "Just staring off into space."

He was telling the truth, in a way. He had always been fascinated by books and movies about outer space and distant planets. Sometimes he even dreamed about a strange world with a giant red sun.

He didn't know why.

CHAPTER EIGHT

Four months later . . .

A junior-league soccer game was underway in the community field in Smallville. The crowds in the bleachers cheered enthusiastically as Whitney scored another goal, putting his team ahead. He whooped in celebration.

"Show-off," Clark muttered.

He watched enviously from the Kent farm many miles away. The roof had been fixed for months, but his parents still wouldn't let him join a team with the other kids. While

Whitney and the rest enjoyed their game, Clark was stuck in an empty field all by himself, viewing the game with his telescopic vision. He listened to the cheers of the crowd. Everybody sounded like they were having a great time.

It wasn't fair.

Then again, he admitted, it wouldn't really be fair for him to play against ordinary kids, not with all he could do. He could win every game if he wanted to, without even trying. The only person he could really compete against was himself.

Like today.

It was a warm, muggy spring afternoon, and Clark felt like seeing what he could do. The fields had already been harvested, so there was open space all around him. He scanned the vicinity for miles around to make sure no one else was nearby, then kicked the soccer ball he'd brought with him.

The ball shot across the fields like a missile, going over a hundred miles an hour. Clark chased after it, running even faster than the ball. No ordinary person could have caught up with the ball, let alone pass it, but Clark intercepted the ball and kicked it back the way it had come. He ran at full speed to meet the ball a few miles away and kicked it back across the fields again.

"I'd like to see Whitney do that!" he said.

He raced back and forth across the dusty fields, playing soccer with himself. He looked like a blurry streak zipping across entire acres in a matter of seconds. Once, the ball almost got past him, but he managed to block it before it went zooming all the way to Smallville. He headed it back toward the farm. The sturdy rubber ball felt like a party balloon against his forehead.

I should try kicking around a bowling ball, he thought. *That might be more of a challenge.*

Clark enjoyed testing his abilities, even if there was no one around to cheer him on. It wasn't often that he got to be himself this way. It felt as natural as breathing. The ball went flying over the farm and Clark jumped

over the barn to chase after it, clearing the large red
building in a single bound.

If only Lana and the others could see him now!

He had to be careful not to kick the ball too hard.
He had destroyed a couple of balls that way, before he
got more control of his strength. Another ball had ended
up crashing through a window at an office in town.
Nobody had ever figured out where it had come from.

Clark still felt guilty about that.

He played hard for an hour or so, working up
a sweat and an appetite. Stopping for a snack, he
fished a can of beef stew from his backpack. He hadn't
brought a can opener, but that didn't matter. He pried
off the lid with his bare fingers and crumpled it into a
tiny wad of metal. A quick burst of heat vision heated
the stew.

"Who needs a stove?" he said.

The tasty stew hit the spot. Clark sat back and
enjoyed his meal. Despite everything, this was turning
out to be a pretty good day.

But Kansas weather was known for its unpredictability. All at once, the wind whipped up and thunder boomed in the distance. Jumping to his feet, Clark saw a tremendous thunderstorm bearing down on him. Lighting flashed across the sky as billowing black clouds appeared on the horizon, blowing rapidly across the sky. The thunderclouds resembled huge floating anvils. The storm looked like it was a big one.

And it was almost here!

CHAPTER NINE

"Clark! Clark!"

He heard his mom calling his name, back by the farmhouse. Clark wasn't particularly afraid of the storm, since almost nothing could hurt him, but he didn't want his mother to worry. He gulped down the last of his stew and grabbed his soccer ball. It looked like his solo soccer game was over.

No point in getting drenched, he thought.

He raced back to the house at super-speed, leaving a

large plume of dust behind him. He beat the storm by only a minute or two. Ominous dark clouds rolled toward the farm. Thunder boomed nearby. Lightning flashed.

"Here I am, Mom!" he said, appearing beside her. He put down his ball. "Need any help?"

She was busy yanking the laundry off the clothesline. Before she could even answer, Clark rescued the rest of the laundry and stuffed it, neatly folded, into her basket. He took the heavy basket from her.

"Oh my," she said. "Thanks, dear!"

A few yards away, Clark's dad tugged open the painted metal doors to the storm cellar. He scowled as he looked up at the approaching tempest.

"I don't like the looks of this," Jonathan said. "We'd better take cover."

Kansas storms could be dangerous. Heavy wind, hail, lightning, and floods had been known to catch people by surprise. Anybody who grew up in these parts knew just how powerful and unpredictable nature could be. It didn't pay to take chances when a storm hit.

Finding shelter was the smart thing to do.

Martha lingered in the backyard. "Shelby!" she called out. "Shelby!"

Clark realized that the dog was nowhere to be seen. "He's not inside?"

His mom shook her head.

"The thunder frightened him," she explained. "He ran off before I could catch him."

Shelby had never liked thunder. As a puppy, he'd always hid under Clark's bed during storms—or down in the storm cellar with the rest of the family.

"Which way?" he asked anxiously.

Martha pointed off toward the west. Acres of farmland stretched to the horizon. "That way, I think!"

The storm bore down on them. The sky went dark as thick black clouds obscured the sun. The temperature dropped dramatically. Hail rained down from the clouds. A fist-sized chunk of ice struck a window, cracking the glass. Another hailstone headed straight for Martha, but Clark jumped in the way so that the ice shattered harmlessly against his skull instead. It didn't hurt a bit.

"Shelby!" he shouted. He put down the laundry and cupped his hands around his mouth. "SHELBY!"

"We'll have to look for him later!" Jonathan called out. He stood by the cellar doors, beckoning to Martha and Clark. Wooden steps led down to the cellar. "We need to get inside!"

"NO!" Clark decided. "I'm not going to leave him out in the storm!"

Shelby was his best friend. He couldn't let the dog face the storm alone. What if Shelby got lost or injured—or worse? Clark would never forgive himself if something happened to his pet.

"I'm going to find him!"

"Clark, wait!" His mother tugged on his arm. "It's too dangerous!"

"Not for me," he said.

There wasn't time to argue about it. Clark dashed away from the farm, even as his parents raced down into the storm cellar. Clark wasn't worried about his parents. He knew they would be safe from the storm. They might be mad at him later for running off like this, but he couldn't worry about that now. He needed to find his dog.

"SHELBY! COME HERE, SHELBY!"

The storm was getting stronger and more ferocious by the moment. Torrential sheets of rain blew against him. Within seconds, he was soaked to the skin. Water dripped from his hair and ran down his back. Dusty fields turned into seas of mud. Howling winds carried his words away. The thunder tried to drown him out.

"SHELBY!"

The hail got worse. Icy missiles bombarded him, bouncing off his head and shoulders. Any normal person would be black and blue by now, maybe even knocked out cold, but Clark kept searching for the lost dog. He impatiently wiped the rain from his eyes. Even with his special vision, he could barely see where he was going. He didn't see or hear Shelby anywhere.

"Come on, boy! Where are you?"

He remembered the dog whistle in his pocket. In theory, the whistle was pitched too high for human ears, but Clark heard it just fine. He hoped Shelby would, too. Clark blew hard on the whistle. Shelby had been trained to come running when he heard it. The high-pitched whistle hurt Clark's ears.

He put down the whistle and waited.

Shelby didn't come.

"Dang it, you crazy dog. Can't you hear me calling?"

Part of him hoped that Shelby had just found a safe place to hide from the storm. He briefly considered giving up and turning back, at least until the storm had passed, but he kept on searching. Shelby could be in trouble. Clark wasn't going to stop looking until he knew his friend was safe.

"HERE, SHELBY! COME!"

He listened for an answering bark, but didn't hear anything. His worried blue eyes scanned the landscape, but he didn't know where to look. Wind and rain blew against his face. Hail kept pelting him, sometimes right in the eyes. He kept them open anyway. A little ice couldn't hurt them. He spun around, looking all about. He didn't know which way to go. Shelby could be anywhere by now.

If only there were some way to find him!

A row of giant transmission towers ran across the fields and farmland, supporting miles of high-voltage power lines. An idea occurred to Clark, and he jumped to the top of the nearest tower, which was more than a hundred feet off the ground.

Maybe he could spot Shelby from way up high?

If anything, the wind was even stronger high above the ground. Clark grabbed the solid steel support frame to keep from being blown off the tower. Lightning flashed overhead, accompanied by a deafening clap of thunder. Clark suddenly realized that standing on top of a metal tower in the middle of a thunderstorm was probably a very bad idea.

CHAPTER TEN

A sizzling bolt of lightning shot down from the sky,
striking Clark directly in the chest. Everything went white
for a minute as a powerful electric shock jolted Clark from
head to toe. His hair stood on end, and his skin tingled.
Stunned, he tumbled off the tower and fell dozens of feet
to the ground below, crashing down into the mud at the
base of the tower.

"Whoa," Clark said.

Dazed, he needed a few minutes to recover. Clark

had never been hit by lightning before and his head was ringing. Smoke rose from his singed clothing, before the pounding rain put out the fires. He wondered how he was going to explain the charred fabric to his folks.

I'll figure that out later, he thought. *After I find Shelby.*

Clark stumbled to his feet. Despite having been struck by lightning, he was still determined to bring his friend home. It wasn't safe out in the storm for anyone, let alone a lost dog. Since he didn't know where to look, he closed his eyes and *listened* instead. The nonstop thunder and wind made using his super-hearing trickier than usual, but Clark tried to tune out the distracting noises.

"Focus," he whispered to himself. "Listen."

At first, all he heard was the furious storm, raging all around him, but then he heard, very faintly, a dog barking frantically. Clark's heart jumped at the sound. He recognized the familiar bark right away.

It was Shelby!

He wiped the mud from his eyes and turned them toward the distant barking. Concentrating hard, he peered through the blinding wind and rain. His telescopic vision zeroed in on a nearby river, only a few miles away, which had burst its banks and was flooding over the countryside. Squinting, Clark spotted Shelby in the river, being tossed about by the frothing white water. He guessed that the terrified dog had been carried off by a flash flood caused by the sudden downpour. Poor Shelby probably had no idea how he'd ended up in the river.

The dog paddled helplessly, unable to escape the current. Loose debris, also captured by the flood, bobbed in the froth as well. Shelby tried to scramble onto a floating wooden crate, but slipped back into the water. An upside-down canoe nearly collided with the dog before being tossed in another direction. It was a miracle that Shelby hadn't drowned already, but the river was rapidly carrying the terrier downstream, away from Clark. The boy knew he had to move quickly to save his friend.

"Hang on, Shelby!" Clark shouted. "I'm coming!"

CHAPTER ELEVEN

Clark ran to the flooded riverbank in record time. Without hesitating, he dived into the churning water. The coldness of the water did not bother him. Clark was immune to extremes of temperature. He had never gotten frostbite or even a sunburn. And he was already soaked by the rain.

He kicked off his shoes and swam at top speed toward Shelby, throwing up a huge tail of spray behind him so that he looked like a speeding motorboat. Coming within

reach of the thrashing dog, Clark grabbed Shelby
and clutched the terrier to his chest. The panicky dog
squirmed in his arms, but Clark held on to him tightly,
making sure to keep Shelby's head above the water.

"It's okay, boy," he murmured. "I've got you!"

But now what was he supposed to do? The white
water tossed them both about, making it hard for Clark
to get his bearings. Broken wooden planks, garbage
cans, street signs, litter, tree branches, and other debris
were being washed along with them. Just in time, Clark
saw a log barreling through the water toward them.
He turned his back toward the log so that it would hit
him and not Shelby. The heavy log smashed to splinters
against Clark's indestructible body. Harmless strips of
timber washed past the boy and his dog.

That was close, Clark thought.

The water was too deep to touch bottom, so Clark
couldn't just jump out of the river. His feet had nothing
to push off against. He struggled to stay right side up
and keep Shelby from drowning. The squirming dog

was hard to hold on to. Foaming water splashed against Clark's face. He sputtered and spat out a mouthful of river water. His eyes searched desperately for some way out of the river.

He spotted a tall elm tree growing at the edge of the river. The tree was already leaning out over the water, but its branches looked too high up to reach—unless he did something to fix that.

Clark's eyes glowed like red suns. Twin laser beams cut through the base of the tree, causing it to fall across the river directly in front of Clark and his dog. Holding on to Shelby with one arm, Clark grabbed the slippery tree trunk and started to pull himself to shore. He hoped that the toppled tree trunk wouldn't be carried away before he made it to safety.

The furious current tried to tear Clark loose from the fallen tree, but he hung on and slowly dragged himself out of the river. By the time they were finally clear of the floodwaters, he was completely covered in mud. Clark let go of the tree trunk and scrambled to his feet. Shelby whimpered in his arms.

"See," Clark said. "I told you we'd be okay."

Shelby was looking happier already. Excited to be rescued and reunited with Clark, the dog enthusiastically licked the boy's face.

"Yeah, yeah," Clark laughed. "I'm glad to see you, too!"

The storm was finally letting up a little, although the rain was still coming down in buckets. Relieved to have recovered his dog, Clark figured it was time to head back home. His parents were probably worried about them both.

"What do you say?" he asked Shelby. "You ready to get out of the rain?"

The dog barked in agreement.

Clark scooped Shelby up in his arms, planning to run all the way back to the farm, but before he could take another step, he suddenly heard a human voice crying out somewhere nearby.

"Help me!" the voice shrieked. "Somebody help me!"

CHAPTER TWELVE

"Please, somebody help me!"

The voice sounded familiar, but Clark couldn't place it right away. Sheer terror distorted the voice, which obviously belonged to somebody in serious trouble. Clark couldn't turn away from that, even if it risked giving away his secret. He had to help if he could.

Shelby barked in his arms, anxious to go home. Clark looked around for a safe place to stow the dog, but didn't see one nearby. He didn't want to abandon Shelby by the river, so he raced back to the farm at super-speed. It took him less than a minute to reach the farm and yank open the storm cellar doors. He put the dog on his feet and prodded him down the steps.

"There you go, boy. Stay!"

His parents stared up at him from the cellar. His mother gasped in relief. "Clark! You're back!"

"Sorry," Clark said quickly. "Gotta run!"

"Wait!" his dad called out. "Where are you going?"

There was no time to explain. Clark spun around and zoomed back the way he came. He could still hear that frightened voice screaming out loud.

"Somebody! Anybody! Help!"

Clark finally recognized the voice.

It was Whitney!

The bully wasn't Clark's favorite person, but that didn't matter now. Clark followed the sound of Whitney's voice to a flooded country road beside the river. A flash flood had washed the car into a ditch, which was rapidly filling up with water. Whitney and his dad were trapped inside the car, unable to get out. Mr. Fordham was slumped over the wheel, knocked out by the crash. Whitney was stuck in the passenger seat, which was wedged against the side of the ditch. Water was rushing into the car. It was already up to Whitney's neck and rising. He looked scared to death.

"HELP ME! I CAN'T GET OUT!"

A thick layer of mud covered Clark's face and clothes. He smeared some more mud on, just to be safe. He hoped that would be enough to conceal his identity. With any luck, Whitney would be too freaked out to recognize him.

"Hold on!" Clark hollered, disguising his voice. "I hear you!"

He dashed to the ditch. The water was waist-deep and rushing fast, but Clark didn't let the current knock him off his feet. He splashed through the water to get to the drowning car. He shoved the whole car to one side so that he could get at the passenger-side door. He tried the handle, but the dented steel door didn't budge. Clark saw that it had been warped by the crash. It was jammed shut.

That was no problem.

He yanked the stuck door open with one hand, practically ripping it off its hinges. He tore Whitney's seat belt off and tugged the boy from the car. He hauled Whitney up onto a muddy rise above the ditch. Whitney coughed up a mouthful of water. His face was white as a sheet.

"My—my dad," he sputtered. "He's still trapped in the car!"

Clark hadn't forgotten about Mr. Fordham. Jumping back into the ditch, he waded quickly through the rushing water. He reached into the flooding car and pulled out the unconscious adult. There was a nasty bruise on the man's forehead, but he was still breathing. Clark quickly inspected Mr. Fordham's head with his X-ray vision.

He didn't see any fractures or internal bleeding.

"Your dad's going to be okay," Clark told Whitney. He carried the limp figure to safety and laid him down on the rise next to Whitney, who was pale and shaking like a leaf. Clark looked his classmate over. "Are you all right?"

"I . . . I think so," Whitney said. He wasn't acting at all like the bully Clark was used to. Whitney was just a scared, badly shaken kid right now. He glanced back and forth between his dad and the car, which was now completely filled with water. He gulped as he realized how close he had come to drowning. Tears filled his eyes. "We tried to drive through the water, but it was too deep. My dad lost control of the car. . . ."

Mr. Fordham began to stir. He murmured weakly. "Whitney?"

The rain was definitely letting up. Clark knew he needed to get away before Whitney calmed down enough to recognize him. There was a phone back at the farmhouse. If he called 911, a police car or ambulance could be here in minutes.

"Wait right here," Clark promised. "Help is on the way."

"Huh?" Whitney squinted at the mud-covered figure before him. "Are you going somew—"

Clark was gone before he could finish the sentence.

CHAPTER THIRTEEN

The sky was clear the next morning. You'd never know there had been a violent thunderstorm less than twenty-four hours ago.

Clark waited nervously for the school bus. What if Whitney had recognized him after all, or figured it out later on? Clark and his folks had watched the TV news the night before, but there had been nothing about a mysterious stranger rescuing Whitney and Mr. Fordham, only a short bulletin about a local father and son who had survived a car accident during the flood. According to the news, both Whitney and his dad were okay.

Clark had been glad to hear it, but he was still worried about his secret. He had barely slept at all last night. How could he explain everything he had done yesterday, like ripping open the car or hearing Whitney's cries from miles away? What if Whitney had told the police the whole story?

The bus approached the Kent farm, where Clark was standing alone out by the road. He braced himself as the bus came to a stop, and he climbed inside. Maybe Whitney had skipped school today? Clark could live with that. It would give him more time to think up a plausible excuse or explanation.

But no such luck. Clark spotted Whitney sitting in the middle of the bus, surrounded by his buddies. Clark lowered his head, hoping to avoid eye contact with the other boy. He crossed his fingers.

Here we go, he thought. *Maybe.*

He walked right past Whitney, who didn't even

glance in Clark's direction. He was too busy bragging to the other kids.

"So you really saved your dad's life?" Pete Ross asked. Pete was Whitney's best friend and accomplice.

"Absolutely!" Whitney said. "After the car went off the road, my dad hit his head and got knocked out. So it was up to me to save us both. It wasn't easy, but I pried the door open and dragged my dad to safety. He would have drowned for sure if not for me!"

Clark couldn't believe his ears. Was Whitney really taking credit for saving his dad?

"Wow!" Lana said, impressed. "Weren't you scared?"

"Nah," Whitney lied. "The water was pouring into the car, but I kept my head and did what needed to be done. Times like that, you find out what you're really made of . . . and I have nerves of steel."

"How did you get the car door open?" Pete asked. "I heard it was all warped out of shape."

"Umm, adrenaline, I guess," Whitney said. "You know how it goes. When you're in danger, sometimes you just find the strength to save the day."

"Wow," Lana said again.

Clark bit his tongue. He knew he should be glad that Whitney was lying about what happened, and not mentioning the muddy Good Samaritan who really came to the rescue, but it bugged Clark that Whitney was getting all the credit for being a hero.

It wasn't fair.

Whitney kept bragging about his heroic feat all the way to school. Clark noticed that the story kept getting bigger and more impressive each time Whitney told it. Clark guessed that the car would be underwater and on fire by lunchtime.

Oh well, he thought. *At least nobody got hurt.*

And Shelby was safe and happy at home again.

The bus stopped, and Whitney swaggered down to the sidewalk in front of the school. A brand-new skateboard was tucked under his arm. It was black with fiery red racing stripes.

"Check this out," he bragged, showing off the

board. "My dad got me this for saving his life!"

"Pretty cool!" Pete said.

"You bet!" Whitney was obviously enjoying all the attention. He plopped the board down onto the pavement. "Watch these moves!"

Clark couldn't resist teaching Whitney a lesson. Too quickly for anybody to see, twin bursts of heat vision shot from Clark's eyes, melting the skateboard's polyurethane wheels. Whitney hopped onto the board, which skidded against the pavement before flipping over. Caught by surprise, Whitney tumbled backward onto his rear end.

The other kids laughed.

"Cool move, Fordham!" someone shouted. "Let's see that one again!"

"Hey!" Whitney scrambled to his feet, wincing slightly. He flipped the skateboard over and saw that the rear wheels were now just gooey blobs. Confused, he touched one of the wheels and then yanked his hand back. "Ouch!"

He sucked on his burned finger.

Clark tried not to smirk too much. He knew that his parents probably wouldn't approve of him using his powers like that, but Whitney had it coming. Clark figured that, after saving Whitney's life, he deserved to have a little fun at the bully's expense. He was only human . . . sort of.

He grinned all the way to class.

CHAPTER FOURTEEN

Three years later . . .

Now thirteen years old, Clark wandered aimlessly
through the county fair, bored and looking for
something to do. His mom was over at the baked-
goods tent, hoping to win another blue ribbon for
her homemade rhubarb pie, while his dad was busy
checking out the latest farm equipment on display. Clark

figured he saw enough tractors and combines every day, so he was in the mood for something a little more fun.

He just wasn't sure what.

A bustling crowd filled the fairgrounds, enjoying the various displays and attractions. The cool autumn air smelled of apple cider, corn on the cob, and livestock. Open barns and stalls held prize cattle, goats, sheep, hogs, and rabbits. The hobby hall showed off handmade quilts, needlepoint, and other crafts. A local country music band performed in an outdoor gazebo, their amplified tunes booming all over the fair. Clark thought they weren't bad.

He felt a little guilty about not joining his dad, but he had already decided that he didn't want to be a farmer when he grew up. He still wasn't sure what he wanted to do with his life—and his special abilities—but he guessed that it didn't involve raising crops. Farming was a proud tradition, but you didn't need superpowers to be a good farmer. He felt that he had been given his abilities for a reason.

But what?

"Step right up!" a fair worker called out, distracting Clark. "Everybody, try the corn maze!"

The maze, which covered more than five acres, offered fairgoers of all ages a chance to get lost in rows of tall cornstalks, laid out in a complicated pattern full of confusing twists and turns. The stalks were too high to see over and too close together to see through, unless you were Clark, of course. He briefly considered walking the maze, but decided that it would be too easy to cheat with his X-ray vision. He could see straight through the maze if he wanted, so he turned toward the pumpkin bowling instead.

"C'mon, young man," an old guy called to Clark from the game. He was a volunteer working for the fair. "Give it a try!"

An outdoor bowling alley had been set up next to a bin of big orange pumpkins. The idea was to roll an actual pumpkin down a lane to knock over the bowling pins at the other end. It was harder than it looked.

"Okay," said Clark, who had nothing better to do. "Why not?"

He picked a nice round pumpkin from the bin, pretending to find it heavy. In reality, he could easily have lifted the pumpkin with one finger, but he acted like he needed both hands. Strolling fairgoers paused to watch.

"Hey, look, it's Kent!" a familiar voice intruded.

Clark groaned inside. It was Whitney and his buddies.

"That too heavy for you, loser?" Whitney asked, relishing another opportunity to make fun of Clark. Three years had passed since Clark had secretly saved the bully's life, but Whitney was just as much of a jerk as ever. Some people never changed. "Maybe you need a smaller pumpkin."

Clark was tempted to show off by knocking down all the pins with one throw, but that might attract too much attention. Better to play it safe.

"I can manage, Whitney."

Huffing with phony effort, Clark tossed the pumpkin with both hands. It bounced down the lane, but hit the pins with only enough force to knock over two of the targets. The rest of the pins stayed standing.

"Tough luck," the old guy running the game said. "Better luck next time."

"Is that the best you can do?" Whitney snickered, unimpressed. He swaggered up to the bin and picked out the biggest pumpkin. "Let me show you how it's done."

He hurled the big orange missile down another lane—and knocked over all ten pins. His friends cheered and high-fived him. The game runner gave him a large stuffed teddy bear as a prize.

"Yes!" Whitney gloated. He sneered at Clark. "See, Kent? That's the way you do it!"

Clark fumed inside, but he controlled himself, like his parents had always taught him to. He just stood by as Whitney and his friends shoved past him on their way to the corn maze. Clark heard them laughing and joking at his expense. Whitney ditched the stuffed bear into a trash bin. He hadn't wanted the prize. He had just wanted to beat Clark.

"You didn't do *too* badly before," the pumpkin bowling guy said. He looked like he felt sorry for Clark. "Wanna go again?"

Clark shook his head. Whitney and his pals had taken the fun out of it. Clark was frustrated that he couldn't do his best. He was getting really tired of having to hold back all the time. What was the point of having all these amazing abilities if he didn't get to use them sometimes?

"No, thanks," he said.

Maybe he should just get something to eat instead.

He was debating between a hamburger and a hot dog when he smelled smoke coming from deep inside the corn maze. Screams and shouts attracted his attention. Frightened people, including Whitney and the others, came streaming out of the maze, which had somehow caught on fire.

The fire spread quickly. Bright orange and yellow flames jumped from row to row of dry cornstalks, turning them into eight-foot-tall walls of fire. Clark could feel the heat from the fire on his face. He prayed that nobody was lost in the maze.

"My daughter!" a distraught woman cried out. "Has anyone seen my daughter?"

She tried to rush into the burning maze, but nearby people held her back. It wasn't safe to let anybody back inside the maze. The fire was spreading too fast. Leafy corn husks went up in flames.

"Let me go!" she shouted, struggling to break free. "I have to find Susie!"

A fire alarm sounded, adding to the chaos, but there was no time to wait for the firefighters to make their way through the crowd. As panicked people ran past Clark, jostling him, he searched the maze with his X-ray vision.

Sure enough, he saw a little girl, no more than seven years old, lost in the middle of the burning maze. She was crying, her sobs drowned out by the roar of the flames and the shouts and sirens all around. Smoke filled the maze, causing Susie to cough and choke. She was still alive, but Clark needed to do something fast.

In the confusion, nobody was looking at him. Clark took a deep breath and charged right through a blazing wall of flames into the maze.

Hang on, Susie, he thought. *I'm coming!*

Rows of burning cornstalks stretched all around him. Clark didn't bother trying to navigate the maze's twisted layout. He just smashed through the flaming rows on a straight path to Susie. Red-hot flames licked at his clothes, but they didn't even scorch his indestructible skin and hair. The thick smoke would have blinded anybody else. Clark peered right through it.

He burst through a wall of fire to reach Susie. Smoke and soot concealed his identity, not that the terrified little girl was likely to recognize him.

Susie ran toward him, crying.

"It's okay," Clark said. "I've got you!"

He scooped her up into his arms and looked around for the safest way out. He had bulldozed a path behind him, but flames and smoke were already filling the gaps. That was no problem for him, but Susie was another story. She was already having trouble breathing. He needed to get her away from the fire as quickly as possible.

He lifted his gaze toward the sky. The safest way out was up.

He bent at the knees and then jumped for the sky. A powerful leap carried them high above the burning maze into the clear air above the smoke. They touched down in a dining area outside the maze. Empty picnic tables and benches had been abandoned by frightened fairgoers.

"Are you okay?" Clark asked.

"Uh-huh," Susie answered. "I think." Coughs punctuated her words, but she was already breathing better. A quick X-ray scan of her lungs revealed no serious damage. She stared wide-eyed at Clark, whose face and clothes were blackened by soot and ash.

"Who are you?"

"Just a friend," Clark said.

A crowd of people ran toward them. Clark realized that he needed to get away before someone recognized him, soot or no soot. He spotted Susie's mother in the crowd and hastily handed the little girl back to her mom.

"Here you go, ma'am," he said, disguising his voice. "Safe and sound."

"Susie!" the mom said, clutching the girl. Tears of happiness streamed down her face. "Thank heavens!"

Clark didn't stick around to be thanked. He dashed back into the fiery maze, figuring that nobody in their right mind would follow him there. Unfazed by the raging inferno, he took a moment to scope out the situation.

What next?

His X-ray vision confirmed that nobody else was trapped inside the blazing maze, but the crisis wasn't over yet. The fire threatened to spread beyond the maze to the rest of the fair, with its closely packed tents and barns. Cows and horses and the other livestock were already panicking. Clark worried about his mom and dad and the hundreds of other people and animals attending the fair. What if they didn't get away in time?

A water tower rose over the fairgrounds not far away. Clark suddenly knew what to do.

Hidden by smoke and fire, he leapt out of the maze and landed at the base of the water tower. Sturdy steel legs, more than 150 feet tall, supported a massive steel tank holding five hundred thousand gallons of water.

That should be enough, Clark thought.

He scanned the fairgrounds to make sure everyone was out of the way. Fortunately, people were running away from the burning maze, not toward it. Firefighters struggled to make their way through the stampede of people to get to the fire. Clark could tell that they weren't going to make it in time.

It was up to him.

Lining up the maze with the tower, he leaned against one leg of the tower and pushed. The huge,

water-filled tower was heavier than anything he had
ever tried to move before, but he put his shoulder
against the unyielding metal leg and pressed into it with
all his super-strength. He grunted from the exertion. This
wasn't like pretending to have trouble lifting a pumpkin.
He really was straining this time. He gritted his teeth.

At first, the tower refused to budge, but then it
began to give way. Once the tower started to tip,
gravity did the rest. The huge steel legs tore loose from
their concrete moorings and the entire tower toppled
toward the fairgrounds.

Look out below!

The water tower crashed down on the flaming maze.
The giant tank burst, flooding hundreds of thousands of
gallons of water onto the fire, extinguishing it instantly.
An enormous plume of steam rose high into the sky.
Cheers rose from the firefighters and civilians.

The fair had been saved!

But nobody could know who had put out the fire and
rescued Susie. Clark zipped away from the shattered

foundations of the water tower before anyone could come to investigate. The tower's timely collapse would have to be a mystery.

Clark wondered how the papers would explain it.

Wiping the soot from his face, he hurried back to the fairgrounds, where he was relieved to find his parents safe and sound in a crowded parking lot outside the fair, which had been closed to the public. Hundreds of people were milling around, watching all the excitement. Others were driving away as quickly as they could. Jonathan and Martha were waiting by their truck. They were relieved to see their son.

"Clark!" His mom ran forward and hugged him. "We've been looking for you everywhere!"

He wasn't sure if he should admit to what he had been up to.

"Um, I was kind of busy."

"I'll bet," Jonathan said knowingly. He eyed Clark's singed clothing and offered Clark his own jacket to cover up the burned fabric. He smiled at Clark. "Good work, son. I'm proud of you."

Clark realized that his father had figured out the truth. "You're not mad at me for using my abilities?"

"From what I gather, you saved a little girl—and maybe the entire fair." Jonathan shrugged. "Hard to find fault with that." He lowered his voice and glanced around to make certain they wouldn't be overheard. "Nobody saw you, right?"

Clark shook his head. "I don't think so. There was a lot of smoke and confusion. Everyone was running from the fire."

"Good." Jonathan placed a hand on Clark's shoulder. "You're getting older now. We're going to have to trust you to use your own judgment sometimes." He contemplated the smoldering remains of the fire, which was no longer a threat to the flooded fairgrounds. Charred corn husks and ashes were being washed away by muddy streams of water. Livestock were being led away safely. Jonathan nodded in approval. "Seems to me you made the right call here."

"I know you did," his mom added. "And I'm sure that little girl's mother would thank you if she could."

Clark was warmed by his parents' praise. He felt proud of himself, too, and pleased that he had been able to use his special abilities to prevent a tragedy, just like he had when he rescued Whitney from that flood years ago. Using his powers this way felt right, like it was what he was always meant to do. He suddenly felt very grateful for his superpowers. He was lucky to have them.

He still didn't know why he was different from everybody else, but he finally knew what he wanted to do with his life, and why he had been given his abilities.

He was here to help people.

CHAPTER FIFTEEN

Clark was sitting on the back porch, gazing up at the stars, when his father found him. Jonathan looked at the boy thoughtfully. He nodded to himself, as though making a decision.

"What is it, Dad?" Clark asked.

"I think it's time," his dad said.

Clark could tell that this was serious. "Time for what?"

"Time to give you some answers . . . about why you

can do the things you can."

Clark jumped to his feet, unable to believe his ears. For as long as he could remember, his parents had been telling him that he would understand why he was so different when he was older, but that day never seemed to come. He had been waiting for this moment for his entire life.

"Tell me!" he said eagerly. "I have to know. How can I do all these things? Why aren't I like everybody else?"

"Come with me," Dad said. "I'll show you."

He led Clark to the old threshing barn behind the house. It was dark out, so he used a flashlight to guide the way. The run-down wooden building had been replaced by a larger barn when Clark was just a child. He had always been told to keep away from it because it wasn't safe anymore. Jonathan unlocked the gate and asked Clark to open it. Rusty hinges squeaked as Clark forced the stubborn gate open. As far as he knew, nobody had set foot in the old barn for years.

What had his folks been hiding there?

The ground floor of the barn was filled with forgotten junk and cobwebs. Jonathan pushed aside an old wheelbarrow to reveal a basement door in the floor. Clark tugged open the door. Wooden steps led down to an old root cellar that Clark hadn't even known about. He looked at his dad in confusion.

"It's down there," Jonathan said.

Clark hurried down the steps. Unlike his dad, he didn't need a flashlight to see by. His eyes widened at the sight of a large object, about the size of a tractor, resting on the floor of the cellar. A dusty tarp covered the object, which looked as though it had not been disturbed in who knew how long.

"Is this it?" he asked.

His dad flicked a switch. A solitary lightbulb lit up the cellar.

"Go ahead," Jonathan said. "Check it out."

Clark didn't bother with his X-ray vision. He yanked off the tarp, exposing a bizarre space capsule that looked like nothing that NASA had ever launched into orbit. Scorch marks blackened the curved outer shell of the craft, as though it had been through a fire—or maybe the heat of entering Earth's atmosphere. An open hatchway revealed a small, empty cavity inside the capsule. It looked almost like a cradle.

"We found you in this," his dad explained. "It crashed in the fields thirteen years ago, when you were just a baby."

Clark stared at the capsule in shock. His brain struggled to cope with what it meant about who—and what—he really was.

"Where—where did this come from?" he asked.

"Not from Earth," Dad said. "At first we thought maybe the Russians sent it up, but not for long. I had a piece of the hull tested by a scientist at Kansas State University. He couldn't even tell me what it was made of."

"So . . . I'm from outer space?"

"You're our son," Jonathan insisted. "And you always will be. But somewhere you have another mother and father, too. And you must have inherited your special abilities from them."

It was too much to take in all at once. Clark reached out and touched the ship. It didn't feel like metal exactly.

"Do you know where I came from? Why they sent me here?"

Jonathan shook his head. "I wish I knew, son."

"But there must be some clue!" Clark said. His father's staggering revelation had only left Clark with more questions. "Was there anything with me?"

"Just one thing." Jonathan crossed the cellar to a workbench in the corner. Newspaper clippings about UFO sightings were pinned up to a bulletin board over the counter. He opened a drawer and took out a small, black object. "We found this tucked in with you."

He handed the object to Clark. It was a polished black spike, only a few inches long, with the letter "S" printed on it. Clark examined the object, trying to figure it out.

"What does the 'S' stand for?" he asked.

"Beats me," his dad said. "But I figure that belongs

to you now. Who knows? Maybe it's the key to finding out where you came from . . . someday."

That wasn't good enough for Clark.

"But what's this all about?" he asked. "Why am I here?"

"Ultimately, that's up to you, son." His father sat down on the steps. He sounded like he had been thinking about this for a long time. "You have to decide what kind of man you want to be, Clark. Because whoever that man is, he's going to change the world."

His father's words haunted Clark as they locked up the barn again. The mysterious spacecraft remained hidden away, as it had been for Clark's entire life. He couldn't believe that it had been waiting in the old barn all these years.

"You coming inside, son?" Jonathan asked.

Clark shook his head. "Not yet." He gazed up at the stars. "I think I need some time alone."

"I understand," his dad said. "Just remember, Clark.

Your mom and I are always here if you need somebody to talk to."

"I know," Clark said. "Thanks."

His dad went inside the farmhouse, leaving Clark alone with his thoughts. Clark jumped to the top of the old windmill. He often sat up on the windmill when he needed to think. He hadn't worried about falling from it since he was a little kid. And he hadn't needed to climb the ladder.

Now he knew why that fall hadn't hurt him all those years ago. And why he was so different from everybody else.

He wasn't human at all. He was an alien.

A strange visitor from another planet.

It explained a lot, but it was still hard to accept. He felt human enough, and had always thought of himself as human, but what was he really? And where had he come from?

A universe of stars stretched out above him, too far away to touch. He knew that the stars were actually distant suns millions of light-years away. Was he from a planet orbiting one of those stars? Which one?

Clark examined the small black object his dad had found in the spacecraft years ago. He turned it over and over in his hands. His finger traced the capital "S" embossed on the object. He scratched his head in confusion.

"'S' for what?" he wondered aloud. "Space? Star? Something?"

Maybe it wasn't even an "S" at all, but some strange alien symbol that just happened to look like the letter "S." That was possible, too.

What was his real planet like, he wondered, and how far away was it? No wonder he had always been fascinated by the sky and stars. That was where he came from.

But what was he doing on Earth? Why had he been sent here?

That's up to you, his dad had said.

Clark lowered his eyes from the stars and gazed

at Smallville in the distance, and the big wide world beyond. He remembered how right it had felt to rescue Susie from the fire, and even Whitney from that flood years ago. Human or otherwise, he had a chance to make a difference on Earth, no matter what world he had been born on.

His head was full of questions, but one thing was certain.

Clark wanted to be the hero his parents had raised him to be.

CHAPTER SIXTEEN

Superman soared over Metropolis in the aftermath
of the earthquake, thinking back on his early years.
In time, he had learned the truth about himself: that
he was the Last Son of Krypton, sent to Earth by his
birth parents, Jor-El and Lara, so that he would have a
chance for life on a new world. The "S" on his chest,
which now stood for Superman, was also the crest of his
Kryptonian family. He honored their sacrifice by doing
his best every day to protect the people of his adopted

planet. Krypton was gone, but he could still fight for truth and justice on Earth. . . .

The earthquake appeared to be over, but Superman remained on alert. Recovery efforts were already under way in the rubble-strewn streets below. Superman watched with pride as emergency workers and random Good Samaritans came to the aid of their fellow citizens. Metropolis was home to plenty of good people, just like Smallville.

Flames erupted from a broken gas pipe. Scared rescue crews scrambled away from the blaze, fearing an explosion. A bright orange pillar of fire spewed into the sky like the world's biggest blowtorch. Superman could smell the harsh smoke and fumes from more than a thousand feet above. His nose wrinkled.

Better take care of that, he thought.

Superman dived toward the fractured street, which had been split apart by a jagged chasm. Heedless of the flames, he plunged into the chasm to reach the newly exposed pipe. He grabbed both ends of the break and crimped them shut with his bare hands, snuffing out the fire. He squeezed them tighter just to make sure no gas leaked from the broken pipes.

"That should do it," he said.

He leapt from the chasm onto the street, ready for his next task. A grateful police officer hurried to greet him. She was covered in dust and powdered concrete after pulling people from the rubble. Scratches and bruises testified to her efforts.

"Thanks, Superman!" she exclaimed. "The last thing we need right now is a fire raging out of control."

"No problem," Superman said. He glanced around at the wreckage, relieved not to see any casualties amidst all the property damage. "Looks like we've got our work cut out for us."

"We'll rebuild," the cop said confidently. "Metropolis has taken a beating before, but we always come back, bigger and better than before."

Superman admired her attitude. He hoped the worst was over.

It wasn't.

An aftershock rattled the city, causing nearby people to yelp in alarm and brace themselves for more destruction. Concerned, Superman took to the sky and used all his heightened senses to locate the epicenter of the earthquakes. Seismic rumbles called his attention to the harbor and the sea beyond. The tremors seemed to be coming from somewhere deep beneath the ocean floor. Peering out toward the tremors, Superman saw the city was still in deadly danger.

A monstrous tidal wave, churned up by the underwater earthquakes, was surging toward Metropolis. An immense wall of water, more than fifty feet high, was only minutes away from drowning the city.

"Oh, no," Superman cried.

The devastation caused by the earthquake would be nothing compared with what the tidal wave would do. Entire neighborhoods, already damaged by the quake, would be swept away, along with everyone in the vicinity. The subway system would be flooded, drowning all the men, women, and children traveling underground.

"No," Superman said. "Not if I have anything to say about it."

He sped through the air to meet the tidal wave head-on. He streaked above the city's endangered waterfront, which was first in line to be wiped out by the oncoming wave, and zoomed out over the harbor. Warning sirens alerted people to seek higher ground.

The looming wall of water was higher than all but the tallest skyscrapers. It roared like a hurricane and made that long-ago flood in Smallville seem like a mere trickle by comparison. Chopping down a tree with his heat vision wasn't going to be enough this time, Superman realized, and he couldn't halt a tidal wave the way he could a runaway truck or train.

This was going to take everything he had.

He hoped it would be enough.

A cold spray splashed against his face. His eyes flared as brightly as Krypton's giant red sun as

Superman unleashed the full force of his heat vision against the monster wave, tapping into the vast solar power stored in every cell of his body. Earth's hot yellow sun bathed him in its golden light, giving him the strength he needed to save Metropolis from drowning.

Yes, Superman thought. *I can do this.*

A flash of blinding red energy sizzled through the air and struck the giant wave. Millions of gallons of angry white water were vaporized instantly by the crimson beam. Mountains of steam billowed into the sky, away from the city, but wave after wave kept on coming. Even reduced in size, the deadly wave was still big enough to flood Lower Metropolis and destroy the waterfront. Thousands, maybe millions, of innocent people remained in jeopardy.

Superman didn't give up. He channeled the sun's endless energy through his eyes, causing even more of the deadly wave to evaporate. He flew backward, ahead of the shrinking tidal wave, which was now only seconds away from the waterfront. The effort drained his power, leaving him weak and light-headed, but he poured every last bit of his strength into his heat vision. Incandescent red beams boiled away tons of surging water, cutting the relentless wave down to size. Clouds of hot steam blew out to sea like a thick fog. Only Superman's indestructible skin kept him from being scalded alive.

Almost there, he thought. *Just a little more.*

By the time the tidal wave hit the waterfront it was only a tiny fraction of its original size and power. A six-inch wave washed over the evacuated docks and piers before receding back into the harbor. Nothing but a few large pools of water were left behind.

Metropolis was safe!

Exhausted, Superman fell from the sky onto the docks. He couldn't remember the last time he'd felt this tired, but he knew it was worth it. Now Metropolis would have a chance to recover and rebuild after the earthquake.

With his help, of course.

Worried citizens who had fled from the approaching monster wave streamed back onto the docks to check on Superman. They splashed through deep puddles of briny water to reach the weary hero.

"Are you okay?" a burly dock worker asked. He helped Superman to his feet. "I can't believe what you just did. I thought we were all goners for sure!"

"I would never let that happen," Superman promised. "And I'll be fine, thanks. I just need a moment to rest."

The bright yellow sun shone down on him, restoring his strength. Superman stood straighter, already starting to feel like himself again. He was relieved to note that the ground was no longer shuddering. It felt like the quake was finally over.

Spectators ran across and crowded the soggy waterfront to get a better look at the Man of Steel. They applauded and snapped pictures with their phones and cameras. Excited kids squealed and pointed at the hero.

"Way to go, Superman!" somebody called out.

"Good thing you were here!"

"Glad I could help," Superman said sincerely. He mingled with the grateful crowd, shaking hands and accepting hugs. "You can always count on me."

"Smile for the camera!" another spectator shouted.

Superman was happy to do so.

Back in Smallville, when he was growing up, he would have had to run away and hide from the public in order to protect his secrets. But now, at last, he could use his superpowers openly for the good of the entire human race. He almost wished he could go back in time and tell his younger self that everything was going to turn out okay. Once, he had been lonely and confused, not knowing who he really was or why he was here, but not anymore.

The boy from Smallville was now Superman . . . the Man of Steel.

MAN OF STEEL™